OPEN WORLD SQUAD

▶▶ FEED THE BEAST ◀◀

BY MICHAEL ANTHONY STEELE

ILLUSTRATED BY MIKE LAUGHEAD

raintree

a Capstone company — publishers for children

Raintree is an imprint of Capstone Global Library Limited, a company incorporated in
England and Wales having its registered office at 264 Banbury Road, Oxford, OX2 7DY –
Registered company number: 6695582

Designed by Heidi Thompson
Original illustrations © Capstone Global Library Limited 2025
Originated by Capstone Global Library Ltd

978 1 3982 5748 1

British Library Cataloguing in Publication Data
A full catalogue record for this book is available from the British Library.

Printed and bound in India.

CONTENTS

OPEN WORLD

In this online video game, players are free.
Be whatever avatar you want. Team up with
whoever you want. Choose any type of
mission you want! Fantasy adventure, battle
racing, sci-fi, action and more. So log on . . .

Open World awaits!

THE SQUAD

Kai

Screen name: K-EYE
Avatar: Techno-Ninja
Strengths: Supply, Stealth

Kai doesn't like being the centre of attention. He chose a role in OW where he can help others – in the background. His ninja avatar has many pockets to hold the squad's gear. Kai takes the job very seriously. He is quick to rush into a fight and pass out anything the group needs.

Hanna

Screen name:
hanna_banana
Avatar: Elvin Archer
Strengths: Speed,
Long-Range Attacks

Hanna is often busy with her school's drama department. She first joined OW to spend more time with her best friend, Zoe. In OW, she's great with a bow and arrow. Hanna is thrilled to take on a big role during the squad's attacks.

Mason

Screen name: MACE1
Avatar: Rubo-Warrior
Strengths: Leadership,
Close-Range
Attacks

Mason knows the value of teamwork.
So he and his best friend, Kai, teamed up
in OW with cross-country friends Hanna
and Zoe. Mason has a strong avatar. But his
true strength? Acting as squad leader and
bringing together the players' many skills.

Zoe

Screen name: ZKatt
Avatar: Feline Wizard
Strengths: Spells,
Defence

Zoe is a tech wizard and OW expert.
She has been playing the longest out
of the squad. Her avatar's magic and
defence skills help keep the group safe.
Zoe isn't quite a pro gamer. But she's
close! Hundreds of followers watch
her live streams.

CHAPTER 1

ATTACK FROM THE GRAVE

Mason readied his sword and shield. He led
the small group into the dark forest. Moonlight cut
through the trees. It barely lit their path. Mason knew
enemies might be hiding in the shadows. The four
travellers could be attacked at any moment.

> **hanna_banana:** BORING!!! something gonna happen
> soon??

The chat popped up on Mason's computer screen.
He jumped in his chair. His fingers left the keyboard.

In the video game, Mason's robot-headed warrior avatar stopped moving. Mason let out a breath. He was more into the game than he had thought.

Behind Mason's warrior, the cat-like wizard stopped too. Mason guessed Zoe was typing back a reply.

ZKatt: rly? this is a scarier mission

hanna_banana: zzzzzzzzzz

K-EYE: It's plenty scary IMO

That was Kai, Mason's best friend. Kai was the ninja. The third avatar in line. A large bag was slung over his shoulder. He held a sharp dagger.

K-EYE: Light spell Z?

ZKatt: sry dont wanna use spells now. we may need them later

hanna_banana: i can see fine. i DONT see anything 2 shoot tho!!! >:(

And that was Hanna. Her Elvin archer was at the back. She fired an arrow.

FWIT-THUNK! It stuck in a tree.

Mason's fingers raced as he joined the chat.

MACE1: stay ready, u never know wht will happn in OW!

Mason moved his warrior down the path. The others followed. The four avatars were nothing like the thirteen-year-olds who controlled them. But that was the great thing about OW, or Open World. Players could be anything they wanted!

Mason and Kai had begun playing Open World a few months ago. The online video game had lots of genres to tackle. Players could pick sci-fi missions. Racing challenges. Fantasy quests like this one. And much more.

Finishing a quest meant getting character upgrades. Unlocking new levels. Even earning credits to spend at OWM, the Open World Market.

One thing that was true for almost every level? It was best to work as a team.

Mason and Kai had teamed up with Hanna and Zoe. The girls lived across the country. Both were skilled players. But Zoe was pretty much an OW pro. She had lots of online followers and often live streamed play-throughs. She also had lots of gaming knowledge. So she usually chose the squad's missions.

Zoe had been tight-lipped about the goal of this fantasy quest, though.

MACE1: u fnly gonna tell us wht we r up against Z?

ZKatt: no spoilers. but think BIG upgrades

hanna_banana: !!!!

Mason tensed as the path led to an open space. Tombstones littered the ground.

> **K-EYE:** Uh-oh, nothing good happens in a graveyard.

> **ZKatt:** ttly

Mason's screen filled with a cut scene. These video clips often gave players clues. Or showed a new enemy. This was definitely an enemy one.

KRRRISH!

A bony hand burst out of the ground. An arm came next. Then a skeleton warrior pulled itself out of the grave. It held up a wooden shield. It swung a rusty sword.

SHING!

> **hanna_banana:** finally!!!!

> **MACE1:** take it down!

Mason swiped his sword. **SLICE!**

Miss! The undead enemy hit back. Mason's health bar dropped by a third.

Hanna fired an arrow. **FWWIT!** The skeleton held up its shield. Block!

Zoe's avatar raised her furry paws. **CRACK!** Her spell shot lightning at the enemy. No effect!

ZKatt: thats not good

hanna_banana: plan?!!

Mason was about to reply. Then a new cut scene started. A dozen more skeletons clawed out of the ground.

Mason groaned. They couldn't beat one. How could they take down thirteen?

CHAPTER 2

UNBEATABLE UNDEAD

Mason rolled around two skeletons. Then he attacked. **SLICE!**

He hit a skeleton's shield. The wood cracked. But the enemy showed no damage.

The rest of the squad wasn't having much luck. Hanna fired arrow after arrow. Each enemy raised its shield. No damage.

Zoe cast all her spells. She shot energy bolts. Made a mini tornado. Created an earthquake. No damage.

As the ninja, Kai sneaked through the fight. He stole back some of Hanna's fired arrows. His large inventory bag held the squad's gear. So he also gave out health potions to anyone who needed it.

hanna_banana: how do we stop these things??

ZKatt: u wanted a fight

hanna_banana: haha

K-EYE: Only things taking damage are their shields.

MACE1: K is right. think i got a plan

hanna_banana: ???

Suddenly, the door to Mason's bedroom flew open. "*Maaaaaa-son!*" Devon shouted.

Mason glared at his little brother. "What did I say about knocking?"

The eight-year-old rolled his eyes. Devon gave the open door three knocks. "I'm hungry."

"Hang on," Mason said. He turned back to the screen. His avatar just stood there as skeletons attacked! His health was taking a beating.

Mason growled and raised his shield. Then he ran up the path.

"Why are you running away?" Devon asked. He leaned over Mason's shoulder.

Mason pointed. "Out!"

His little brother's lips tightened. Then Devon marched out of the room. He stopped in the hallway. Just outside the door.

Mason sighed.

MACE1: try again later? D is whining 4 dinner. but i got an idea h2 beat the skels

The others left the fight. They ran to Mason.

ZKatt: thought u were tilting for a sec. ttly get the sib drama tho. my little bro Zach can b a pain smtmes 2 :) good luck!

K-EYE: I have to finish homework anyway. Say hey to Devon.

hanna_banana: hope its a good idea M cuz those skels r ruff!!! :(

MACE1: yep. tell u tmrrow. meet at OWM?

ZKatt: k

hanna_banana: bb4n

One by one, the avatars faded away. Mason left the level too. The Open World logo filled his screen.

"Can we eat now?" Devon asked from the hall. He grabbed his stomach. "I'm starving."

Mason sighed again. He had an idea on how to beat the skeletons. But he wished he felt better about his next challenge. Feeding his little brother.

CHAPTER 3

WHAT'S FOR DINNER?

"No," Devon said, shaking his head.

Mason put the meatloaf frozen dinner down.
He raised the other box. This one had a photo of
chicken nuggets. With a side of mac and cheese.

"Nuh-uh," Devon replied. He stuck out his tongue
for good measure. "Blech!"

Mason shrugged. "Listen, dude. This is all we have."
He nodded at the fridge. "It's either one of these or
Mum's leftovers."

"Chicken and rice?" Devon asked.

"Yup," Mason said. "And green beans."

"But we had that last night," his little brother whined.

"That's right," Mason agreed. "That's why they're called *leftovers*."

Devon's shoulders sank. "Okay. Leftovers."

Mason put the frozen dinners back. He pulled out the leftovers. He sighed as he began dishing out the food for his brother and himself.

Their dad had always travelled a lot for work. Then a few weeks ago, Mum had started a new job. She worked some late nights. So, it was up to Mason to make dinner during the week. It was his least favourite chore ever. Getting the food ready wasn't hard. Mason wasn't allowed to use the oven on his own. But he was a microwave pro.

The thing that made the chore so hard? His little brother. Mason could never make Devon happy.

DING!

Mason pulled his brother's plate out of the microwave. Devon slowly stirred the food. He gave it a poke. At last, he took a bite. Instant gross face. Just like always.

"I don't like it," Devon said.

Mason took a bite from his own plate. "You liked it last night."

"Mum makes it better," Devon replied.

Mason shook his head. "That's because it was fresh. This is just warmed up."

"Can you make it better?" Devon asked. "The rice is all crunchy now."

"Just eat it, okay?" Mason asked.

Devon cut off the world's smallest piece of chicken. He chewed as if it were a wad of beef jerky.

"How about the meatloaf?" Devon asked.

"Too late," Mason replied.

"Chicken nuggets?" his sibling added.

Mason glared. "You're eating chicken." Devon opened his mouth to reply, but Mason cut him off. "You don't like it tonight? Think of how it will be tomorrow. Just eat!"

Devon hung his head. He went back to his food.

Mason frowned at his meal. He knew how things would go. Devon would eat a few more bites. He'd say he was full. Then he'd whine that he was hungry when Mum got home.

In Open World, Mason had become the leader of their squad. His friends listened to his ideas. They followed his plans of attack.

But in the real world? Mason couldn't get his brother to eat more than ten mouthfuls of dinner. Mason felt powerless.

If Devon were an enemy in OW, he'd be a beast with endless health. Immune to any kind of attack.

CHAPTER 4

SHOPPING TRIP

Mason logged on the next afternoon. He went straight to OWM. The digital market was huge. It had gear for each part of the game. Gravity boots for sci-fi missions. Horses for Wild West adventures. Vehicle upgrades for racing. And a lot more.

Mason and his friends stopped at a fantasy shop. OWM was outside of the quest. So their four avatars weren't in fantasy costumes. They stood in their normal outfits as the squad chatted.

MACE1: sry for last night. D was being a pain

ZKatt: np

MACE1: cant get thru a level lately w/o him bugging me!!!

ZKatt: maybe let D watch u play?

hanna_banana: ooo ya keep him busy!

MACE1: ez 4 u Z. ur a big streamer. pple always watch u play

ZKatt: just a thought. wrks with Zach sometimes

K-EYE: I like Devon. Thought you guys got along?

MACE1: we do

Mason stared at the screen for a moment. Then he began typing again.

MACE1: we did. ever since mum started her job its just lots of trble at dinner

K-EYE: Sorry. That's tough. Take it easy on Devon k?

MACE1: but i cant cook anything right 4 him, even leftovrs. last night it was the rice! 2 crunchy!!! srsly what am i sposd 2 do

ZKatt: not as good as parents cooking right? same here with Zach

MACE1: yes!!!

hanna_banana: pro tip. old rice + little water = fluffy yummy. mmmmm... try next time before nuking!

MACE1: i will thnks

K-EYE: I know how Devon feels. Leftovers are the worst.

hanna_banana: soooo... 411 on skeletons???

Mason grinned. He was excited to change the subject. He didn't exactly like talking about his struggles with Devon.

MACE1: focus attacks on shields first. destroy them then skels shud be ez

ZKatt: YES! b/c our hits b4 never even got the skels, only damaged shields

K-EYE: Solid plan

MACE1: so load up on spells 2 keep em busy. then i take out shields

hanna_banana: and then my arrows will take out the skels! YAY!!!

K-EYE: Um problem. I can't carry more spells or arrows. My bag is full of extra health potions.

Kai often carried all the squad's gear. That role helped him stay out of the spotlight. Mason's best friend had always been a bit shy.

ZKatt: UPGRADE!!! buy the biggest bag u can. specially 4 whats at the end

hanna_banana: ???

K-EYE: ?

MACE1: big spoiler finally?? so whats at the end of this mission?

Mason leaned closer to the screen. He felt like Zoe was about to whisper a secret.

ZKatt: not much... just a dragon's treasure! all the credits we can carry!

hanna_banana: WHT??? qoolz!!!

K-EYE: A dragon?? The skels are hard enough.

MACE1: get a big bag K and load up on gear.
we'll deal with the dragon when we get there

Mason had tried to sound brave. But really?

He was with Kai. How could they ever defeat a dragon?

CHAPTER 5

BAD NEWS

After the shopping trip, the squad restarted the fantasy level. They marched into the forest. The four avatars wore fantasy outfits again. Mason's warrior was a bit bigger now. They had all chipped in to buy Kai's new bag. But Mason had a few credits left for an armour upgrade.

They came to the graveyard. Cut scene. A skeleton clawed from its grave.

MACE1: u ready Z?

ZKatt: ready!

Zoe's wizard held her paws high. **ZUUURT!**
Light flashed. The skeleton warrior stood stunned.

How did a blinding spell work on something
without eyes? Mason wasn't sure. But it did work!
He attacked the skeleton's shield. By the time the
enemy could see again, its shield was gone.

MACE1: go H!

Hanna shot an arrow. **TUNK!** The enemy
crumbled.

"Yes!" Mason said.

Second cut scene. More skeletons rose up.

ZKatt: WTG!!!!!

K-EYE: YESSSSSS

hanna_banana: >:)

MACE1: lets do this!

The squad stuck to Mason's plan. Zoe cast more blinding spells. Mason hit the nearest skeleton until its shield was gone. Hanna fired an arrow. The undead warrior crumbled. Kai gave Hanna more arrows. Then it was onto the next enemy.

Soon, all the skeletons were gone. They were just piles of bones.

MACE1: gg

ZKatt: :)

hanna_banana: woohoo! :D

K-EYE: Look!

Kai walked to a bone pile. Something was glowing in it. He picked the thing up. A label appeared.

K-EYE: Feral stump root?

MACE1: 4 ur spells Z?

ZKatt: dunno

K-EYE: I'll keep it just in case.

MACE1: yes

hanna_banana: rly? u keep everything K!!!

K-EYE: You never know.

hanna_banana: lol fine keep ur weird root :P

Kai put the mystery item into his new bag. Then Mason led the squad up the path.

Mason was feeling good. Until they reached the top of a hill. A castle stood not far away. Clouds circled its towers. Flashes of lightning lit its dark stones.

MACE1: lemme guess dragons lair?

ZKatt: yep its supposed 2 b in the dungeon

Mason was about to ask if Zoe had heard how to defeat the boss. But his fingers stopped. He saw a hut on the path. And a robed figure holding a staff. Standing by a campfire. Was it a friend or foe?

A cut scene filled Mason's screen.

"More warriors to fight the dragon, I see," the figure said, pulling back the hood. It was an old man. A grey beard stretched down his chest.

"Be warned. All who tried have failed," the man continued. "For the dragon cannot be defeated."

CHAPTER 6

WEB OF FEAR

"I'm *booooooored*," Devon whined just outside Mason's door.

Mason groaned. "Not now, Dev!" He checked the time. "It's not even five yet. You know the deal. I'll finish at six."

Devon didn't say anything. And Mason didn't turn around. But he heard stomps down the hall. Then a door slam.

Mason sighed. He felt a little guilty for shooing away his brother. But things were getting good in OW! He focused back on the cut scene.

"Swords cannot harm the dragon. Nor spells,"
the old man said. "But . . . if it's the dragon's *treasure*
you're after? There might be a way."

MACE1: ok ok

ZKatt: now we r gettin somewhere!

"The beast cannot help but sleep after eating its
favourite meal." The man chuckled. "I know what
you're thinking. But its favourite meal is not warriors
like you. It is a very special stew."

K-EYE: As long as M isn't cooking!

ZKatt: lol

hanna_banana: burn!

MACE1: very funny

"The recipe for Dragon's Stew is simple," the man
said. He poked the campfire with his staff.

He held up four fingers. "You will need titanic spiderweb. Red toadstools. Feral stump root. Centaur tail. The dragon only likes the stew piping hot!"

> **K-EYE:** YES! We already have the root! See this is why I keep everything.

> **hanna_banana:** ok fine, ONE time it helped :)

The old man pointed. Two items on the ground glowed. "I can sell you the toadstools," he said. "And a cauldron to cook in."

The cut scene ended. Kai handed over their last credits. He grabbed the items.

"Good luck," the man said. Then the squad kept moving towards the castle.

> **K-EYE:** Where are the other ingredients Z?

> **MACE1:** ya gotta make that stew

> **ZKatt:** dunno. i only knew about the dragon

hanna_banana: hey M u ever thot about coming up with recipes IRL? for Devon?

Mason blinked. He was so into the game. He had almost missed that the chat was about *his* real-world problem. Slowly, he typed back.

MACE1: no im not a cook. plus theres no ingrednts to use anyway. sunday mum makes a big meal 4 leftovers. then its frozen dinners after

hanna_banana: :(

MACE1: it is what it is. D just likes 2b a pain. he was bugging me already. heads up in case i go MIA

K-EYE: Go easy on him dude.

ZKatt: yeah remember u could just let D watch! wont b that bad, promise

MACE1: i guess. not looking frward to dinner tho

K-EYE: Ever try different spices? I put oregano on everything. So good. Little packets come with our delivery pizza and I hoard them.

hanna_banana: lol just like in the game!!!

K-EYE: True

ZKatt: maybe mix and match stuff? make it different? i do that sometimes when i have 2 cook for Zach

hanna_banana: YES!!! my gran is amazing at that! she can make like 10 things w/ 5 ingredients!!! keeps it interesting :)

Mason moved his avatar down the path. But his mind wasn't on the game now. It was on his friends' ideas. Would Devon go for tricks like that? Their parents' work schedules wouldn't change any time soon. And Mason couldn't turn into a fancy chef. He had to find *some* way to make dinners less stressful.

Mason was deep in thought. So deep, he didn't see it. A shadow moved in the trees.

K-EYE: M!

ZKatt: look out!

WHUMP!

A giant spider dropped down. Mason jumped away just before it landed on him.

Two fangs flashed. Luckily, the spider only bit Mason's shield.

The squad spread out as Mason hit back. The spider blocked with its long legs. But Mason went on hacking. He had to keep the enemy busy. Maybe then the others could get in some hits.

hanna_banana: cant move!

K-EYE: Same!

ZKatt: me 2!

Mason checked on his friends. They were tangled in the spider's web! Thin strands hung all around. The others had walked straight into them.

hanna_banana: HLP M!!!

"Little busy," Mason muttered. He kept attacking the spider.

Suddenly, his bedroom door flew open.

"*Maaaaaa-son!*" Devon shouted.

Mason cringed. The last thing he needed was to face *another* foe.

CHAPTER 7

ONE MORE MEMBER

"Dude!" Mason said. He looked over his shoulder. "What did I say before?"

He looked back at the screen. The spider jumped. It sunk its fangs into Mason's avatar. His health dropped by half.

Another hit like that? He'd be dead. Then the spider would move on. To Mason's trapped squad.

"But it's almost time for dinner," Devon said.

Mason could feel anger boiling up inside him.

"It's only five-thirty!" Mason said. "Can't you just –"

But then he caught himself. One? He'd get into trouble for raising his voice at Devon when Mum got home. And two? It wouldn't solve anything.

Mason took a deep breath. He thought about Zoe's advice from earlier.

"Hey. Why don't you watch me play for a while," Mason said. He kept his eyes on the screen. "Then we can have dinner. Okay?"

Devon sighed. Mason tensed. He was sure he was in for a fight. But he was wrong.

"Whoa! That spider is HUGE," Devon said. He looked over Mason's shoulder. "How are you going to kill it?"

"Don't know yet," Mason replied. He blocked a bite. "But I gotta stay away from those fangs."

"Then attack it from behind?" Devon asked.

Mason raised an eyebrow. "Not a bad idea."

Mason entered a combo attack into his keyboard. His avatar did a double front-flip over the spider. Then he started hacking. One of the beast's legs fell away.

ZKatt: good one!

The spider spun round. But Mason did the same combo move. Flip! Land! Hack! The spider lost a second leg.

"Cool move!" Devon said.

The spider was slower now. Mason hacked. Two more legs gone.

"You're doing it!" Devon shouted.

Mason flipped again. But this time? He leaped high into the air. Spun his sword. Brought the blade down.

SHINK! The spider was finished.

K-EYE: NICE!

hanna_banana: woohoo!!!!

ZKatt: pro gamer moves M!

"That was awesome," Devon said.

"Thanks," Mason said with a grin.

He ran over to his squad. One by one, he freed them from the web.

A glowing item showed up on the ground. Kai grabbed it. A label read: *Titanic Spiderweb.*

K-EYE: YES! Another ingredient!

Devon read the chat. "Ingredient?"

Mason quickly told him about Dragon's Stew. Then his fingers flew over the keyboard.

MACE1: D is here btw. it was his idea to attack the spider frm behind

K-EYE. I ley bud. GG!

hanna_banana: welcome aboard Devon!!!

ZKatt: hello Devon! hih M

MACE1: thnks

Mason didn't think Devon knew what *hih* meant. But Mason had used Zoe's idea of asking his brother to watch. So he *hoped it helped* too.

"What's the next monster going to be?" Devon asked. He grabbed a pillow off Mason's bed. He sat on the floor.

A smile tugged at Mason's lips. "Let's find out."

CHAPTER 8

TIME-OUT

Mason led the squad down the forest path. The castle was closer now. Huge. Dark. Stormy.

"Creepy," Devon whispered.

"Not *too* scary, is it?" Mason asked.

"No way," his brother said. Devon hugged the pillow tighter. He leaned forwards.

Mason felt a wave of relief. It wasn't just because he had beaten the spider. But maybe Devon watching wouldn't be so bad. It was keeping his little brother busy. Just like Zoe had said. Maybe Mason could even finish this level tonight.

Soon, the path came to an old garden. It was full of broken statues.

K-EYE: I bet these things come to life and attack us.

No sooner had Mason read the words when –

SHHHHH-THUNK!

An arrow flew out of the forest! Mason got his shield up at the last second.

Devon jumped. "Whoa!"

"*Shh!*" Mason whispered. But he had goosebumps.

More arrows flew at the squad. They ran behind the statues. Then a cut scene filled Mason's screen.

Galloping hooves pounded the ground. The camera zoomed out. It showed a centaur charging into the garden. The half-human, half-horse drew back its bow. The arrow flew at the camera.

The cut scene faded to gameplay. The centaur ran back into the woods.

hanna_banana: hey bow and arrow is my thing!!!

ZKatt: found the centaur tail huh?

K-EYE: Except it's still attached. And it's fast.

MACE1: ideas?

The centaur galloped out of the trees before anyone could answer. The squad stayed hidden as it fired three more arrows. Hanna fired one back. Her arrow flew past the moving target.

"I got an idea! Can you make a trap?" Devon asked. "Like catch it with rope?"

"It's not that kind of game," Mason said. "I don't think we even *have* rope."

Devon slumped. "Oh."

Mason cleared his throat. "But . . . I can check."

MACE1: any rope K?

K-EYE: Not in my inventory

hanna_banana: rope???

MACE1: D thot of making a trap

ZKatt: great idea!

"Really?" Devon asked.

Mason shrugged. "Maybe Zoe has a plan."

ZKatt: we trap horse guy not with rope but with a time spell. THAT will slow him down

hanna_banana: nice, then we hit em with evrything we got!!!

ZKatt: but i'll b stuck in slomo too when im casting

K-EYE: Sounds risky

MACE1: we got ur back. go 4 it Z!

Zoe ran to the middle of the garden. The centaur burst out of the forest. It drew back its bow. It headed straight for her!

Zoe pulled out a bottle with a clock on it.

WHOOSH! Light flashed. Suddenly, both the centaur and Zoe were moving slowly. Really, really slowly.

MACE1: NOW

The rest of the squad charged out. They attacked the centaur. Mason swung his sword. Hanna fired arrows. Kai jabbed his dagger.

Nothing. The centaur seemed unharmed. It kept pulling back its bow in slow motion.

ZKatt: any time guys!!!

Mason didn't answer. His focus was on the centaur. Swipe! Stab! Jump-chop! His friends kept up their attacks too. Still, the enemy inched closer to Zoe. It was about to fire the critical hit.

ZKatt: guys???

"Go! Go! Go!" Devon shouted. He was jumping up and down.

Mason dropped his shield. He began doing two-handed power attacks.

CHOP! CHOP! CHOP!

Suddenly, the centaur froze completely. Shook. Crumpled to the ground. Victory!

Zoe ended the time spell. She ran to the squad.

hanna_banana: YESSS!!!

MACE1: ru ok Z?

ZKatt: am now thx!

hanna_banana: Z was almost a trophy in a centaur's living room!!!

ZKatt: lol 4 real! horse guys health was insane

K-EYE: A trap was the best way to beat him no doubt. GG D!

Mason smiled at his little brother. "Yeah.
Good idea, Dev."

"Thanks!" Devon replied with a grin.

The centaur faded away. Only one part was left.
Kai grabbed the glowing tail.

K-EYE: That's all the ingredients!

hanna_banana: yay!!!! :)

MACE1: next stop, the dragon

CHAPTER 9

DINNER FOR ONE

The squad headed for the castle. Mason turned to his little brother. Devon was still standing.

"So what do you think?" Mason asked. "It's just about six. Want to stop? Have dinner?"

"And miss the dragon?!" Devon said. "No way! We're so close!"

"You sure you don't want to go and get a snack?" Mason asked.

Devon shook his head. "Nuh-uh!"

Mason grinned. "Thanks, dude."

Devon sat back on the floor. He scooted closer. Then Mason returned to the game.

The squad came to the castle. The main archway was crumbling. Rubble was scattered across the path. The stone walls were burnt black.

hanna_banana: yikes the dragons place is almost messier than my room!!!

K-EYE: LOL

ZKatt: yeah almost

hanna_banana: HEY

The players found a set of stairs. It led down into darkness.

MACE1: ready 2 face the dragon?

hanna_banana: born ready!!! >:)

K-EYE: K

Mason went down the stairs. The others followed.

The steps ended at a wide hall. Then a large stone doorway. Cracked wooden beams hung in the opening. Doors had once sealed the dungeon shut. But no longer.

The squad inched closer. Mason gasped. Beside him, Devon sucked in a breath too. The dungeon was huge. But that wasn't what took the brothers' their breath away.

A cut scene showed the dragon itself. The gigantic enemy was sleeping on top of piles of treasure. Gold coins. Gems and jewels. The camera swooped around the beast. Shining red scales covered its body. Jagged teeth jutted from its closed mouth.

The camera zoomed in. It focused on one of the dragon's closed eyes. The eye popped open.

Mason could barely type as the cut scene ended. The dragon was turning. It took a deep breath.

MACE1: TAKE COVR

The squad backed into the hallway.

WHOOOOOSH!

Fire burst through the doorway. The players hugged the hallway wall. But it wasn't enough to keep the squad safe. Their health bars dropped by half.

"Whoa," Devon whispered.

"No kidding," Mason said.

The flames died seconds later. Kai quickly passed out health potions.

K-EYE: That's all, sorry.

hanna_banana: crazy!!!

ZKatt: cant take another hit like that!

MACE1: so lets get cooking

Kai pulled out the cauldron. He dropped the four ingredients into the pot. Zoe cast a fire spell. The pot bubbled. They had Dragon's Stew!

hanna_banana: whos gonna take it in there?!!

K-EYE: Not me

MACE1: me??

ZKatt: relax no ones going. i got 1 spell left...

Zoe's avatar waved her paws. The cauldron rose up. It floated around the corner.

The dragon sniffed. Then its jaws snapped shut around the steaming pot.

CHOMP!

hanna_banana: and???

The dragon opened its mouth again. Mason tensed. But the beast didn't let out a fire blast. It gave a huge yawn. It smacked its lips. Closed its eyes. Rested its head on its mountain of gold.

ZZZZZZZZ!

A snore echoed in the dungeon.

ZKatt: ha total snoozefest!!!

hanna_banana: just like my gdad after a big meal lol

K-EYE: So did it work?

MACE1: only 1 way to find out

Mason stepped into the room. He scooped up some gold.

ZZZZZZZZ!

The dragon kept snoring.

hanna_banana: we did it!!!

"You did it!" Devon echoed.

The rest of the squad ran inside. They quickly filled their packs while the dragon slept. Kai took the longest. He maxed out his extra-big inventory bag. It was now stuffed full with dragon's treasure.

hanna_banana: cha-ching!!!

ZKatt: another OW level win! I SO shoulda been streaming this

MACE1: lets meet tomrrw 2 split credits

K-EYE: Where?

MACE1: OWM! time for major upgrades

K-EYE: Yes!

ZKatt: obvs!

hanna_banana: lol you know it!!!

K-EYE: Thanks for the help D!

ZKatt: ditto!

hanna_banana: Yay Devon!!!

Devon read the chat and smiled. Mason grinned too. Having his little brother by his side had been alright. Plus, his squad had defeated the final boss. On their first try.

But Mason had one battle left tonight. He hoped it would be just as successful.

CHAPTER 10

DINNER FOR TWO

Mason held up the two frozen dinners. "Okay, which one? Meatloaf or chicken nuggets?"

Devon rolled his eyes. "What else?"

"More chicken and rice leftovers," Mason said.

His brother's eyes got big. "Three nights in a row?"

Mason put the boxes on the counter. "How about this? Just like in the game, these are our ingredients." He pointed to the different foods on the boxes. "You can use them to make anything you want."

"Really?" Devon asked.

Mason nodded. "Sure. We can even use stuff from Mum's leftovers."

Devon wrinkled his nose. "Crunchy rice."

"Hanna gave me a tip to fix that," Mason said. "Want to give it a try?"

"She did?" Devon asked. "Okay."

Mason microwaved both meals. Then he let Devon pick what would make his dinner. Devon chose the peas that came with the meatloaf. Then two nuggets. A side of mac and cheese. Plus a little rice. Mason put the other food in the fridge. It'd be more ingredients for next time!

Devon dug right in. Mason took a bite of the creation too. Hanna's tip really did work. The rice was fluffy! Almost as fluffy as when Mum had first made it.

"This is good," Devon said with a hint of surprise.

Mason gently punched his shoulder. "I hope so. You helped make it."

Devon gave a wide grin. It was full of macaroni.

"*Duuude*," Mason said. "Gross."

Mason smiled as he watched Devon enjoy dinner. Thanks to his squad's advice, tonight had felt a lot easier. In fact, it had hardly felt like a chore. Dinner had been more like a puzzle to solve. Just like an Open World mission.

"Mum will be home tomorrow," Mason said. "But the next night, we can mix up other ingredients for dinner. Maybe even add some spices?"

"Yeah!" Devon agreed. "Just no spiderweb and centaur tail!"

Mason laughed. "Yeah, it might make you sleepy."

BONUS ROUND

1. How did the squad work together to beat the fantasy level? How did they help Mason out with his little brother problem? Use examples from the text to support your answers.

2. This story is told from Mason's point of view. Try rewriting a scene from his sibling's point of view. What does Devon think about how his older brother is behaving?

3. Think of a time when you were angry or annoyed with a sibling or friend. How did you deal with those feelings? What helped the situation?

4. Imagine you are playing Open World. You are chatting with Mason. Are there any tips you would give Mason for handling times when it's just him and Devon? Or any questions you want to ask him? Write out the chat.

5. In chapter 7, Mason almost yells at Devon. But he stops himself. He takes a deep breath first. How does this help? Has there ever been a time when pausing and taking a deep breath has helped you?

TAKING CARE

In real life, there may not be levels to beat. Or bosses to battle. But it can still be tough. Equip yourself with the tools and knowledge to take care of your mental health. Check out the online resources below. And don't ever be afraid to ask for help from friends, family or trusted adults.

BBC Bitesize:
www.bbc.co.uk/bitesize/articles/zmvt6g8

BBC Children in Need:
www.bbcchildreninneed.co.uk

Childline:
www.childline.org.uk

Health For Teens:
www.healthforteens.co.uk

Mental Health Foundation:
www.mentalhealth.org.uk

NHS Mental Health:
www.nhs.uk/mental-health/children-and-young-adults/mental-health-support/

Young Minds:
www.youngminds.org.uk/young-person/

GLOSSARY

avatar character in a video game, chat room, app or other computer program that stands for and is controlled by a person

centaur mythical creature with the head and chest of a human and the body of a horse

defeat gain a victory over someone or something; to beat

dungeon underground room in a castle

hack cut over and over

ingredient one of the things that is used to make something else

inventory all the things that are with you and are ready to use

mission planned job or task

recipe steps that tell you how to make a certain food

tense if you tense up, your muscles become stiff because you're worried or scared

upgrade something better or newer than the one before

warrior person who is good at fighting and using weapons

wizard person who uses magic

THE AUTHOR

MICHAEL ANTHONY STEELE has been in the entertainment industry for more than 27 years, writing for television, films and video games. He has written more than 120 books for exciting characters and brands, including Batman, Superman, Wonder Woman, Spider-Man, Shrek and Scooby-Doo. Steele lives on a ranch in Texas, USA, but he enjoys meeting readers when he goes to visit schools and libraries across the United States. For more information, visit MichaelAnthonySteele.com.

THE ILLUSTRATOR

MIKE LAUGHEAD is a comics creator and illustrator of children's books, T-shirts, book covers and other fun things in the children's market. He has been doing that for almost 20 years. Mike is also an illustration instructor at Brigham Young University-Idaho, USA. He lives in Idaho with his amazing wife and three wonderful daughters. To see his portfolio, visit shannonassociates.com/mikelaughead

▶▶ READ THEM ALL! ◀◀